Fashion Show Fun

Follow the Glitter Girls' latest adventures!
Collect the other fantastic books in the series:

Caroline Plaisted

Fashion Show Fun

SCHOLASTIC

Scholastic Children's Books,
Commonwealth House, 1-19 New Oxford Street,
London WC1A 1NU, UK
a division of Scholastic Ltd

London ~ New York ~ Toronto ~ Sydney ~ Auckland
Mexico City ~ New Delhi ~ Hong Kong

Published by Scholastic Ltd, 2002

Copyright © Caroline Plaisted, 2002

ISBN 0 439 99457 8

Typeset by Falcon Oast Graphic Art Ltd
Printed and bound in Great Britain by Cox & Wyman Ltd, Reading, Berkshire

2 4 6 8 10 9 7 5 3 1

Chapter 1

It was Saturday afternoon and the Glitter Girls were at Hannah's house. They'd spent a brilliant morning shopping at one of their favourite places, Girl's Dream, and now they were back, the girls were busy discussing all the gorgeous things they'd seen.

"Aren't those matching jeans and jackets just fantastic?" Zoe asked the others.

"Oh, they're so cool!" agreed Hannah. "I love that pink silvery denim!"

"I've never seen material like that, ever!" Meg sighed, wistfully.

"And those T-shirts were fab," said Flo.

"I want all of them!" Charly said dreamily, as she flicked through the pages of a magazine.

"Hey, look," exclaimed Flo, peering over Charly's shoulder. "There's that crop top we saw!"

"Oh yes," said Charly. "Isn't it beautiful? You'd look great in that Flo!"

"Thanks, Charly," said Flo. "I'll just have to save up my pocket money – I want everything in Girl's Dream!"

"Me too!" agreed Meg.

"I don't believe it!" Charly exclaimed suddenly.

"What?" asked Hannah.

"This!" said Charly excitedly, pointing at an article in the magazine.

As the Glitter Girls were leaving Girl's Dream they'd each been given a copy of a special magazine. It was called *Girl's Dream*, just like the shop, and it was packed full of articles about fashion, make-up, music and everything that was sold in the Glitter Girls' favourite shop.

"What is it?" asked Hannah.

Charly had a very big grin across her face.

"They're having a fashion competition!" she said.

★ ♥ ★ ♥ ★ ♥ ★

"Let's see!" the others all cried at once, as they quickly gathered round the magazine that was now spread out on the floor in front of Charly.

Charly read the details of the competition to the others.

"It says that they're holding a fashion show in London!" she said, scanning down to read some more. "And the clothes are going to be all new outfits that haven't been seen before. . ."

"Wow!" said Zoe, imagining how big her wardrobe would have to be if she was lucky enough to own all the clothes in Girl's Dream.

". . .and one of the outfits is going to be designed. . ." Meg continued, ". . .by THE WINNER OF THE COMPETITION!"

"What a cool prize!" said Flo.

"Fantastic!" agreed Hannah.

"What do we have to do?" asked Zoe.

Charly quickly read through the rules and then said, "We've got to design an outfit and then send the design in with a photograph of the designer.

"And the winning outfit will be made up and sold in the shops!" Charly read on. "And as well as the overall winner, thirty runners up will have the chance to model at the fashion show in London!"

"Excellent!" said Flo.

"What's the closing date for entries?" asked Zoe.

Charly looked down at the magazine again. "The 24th – that's two weeks from today!"

"We've got to go for it!" said Flo.

"Flo's right!" agreed Hannah. "We've got to enter!"

"Go Glitter!" the others agreed.

8

"So what are we going to design then?" Zoe asked.

"Bootleg trousers!"

"A mini-skirt!"

"Dungarees!" shouted Flo, Hannah and Charly all at once.

"We've got to agree on one thing if we're going to enter this together," laughed Meg. "So what shall we design?"

"How about a skirt with a matching top and jacket?" suggested Flo.

"But why do we all have to do the one outfit?" asked Zoe. "I mean – can't we all send in our own?"

"I suppose we could. . ." replied Meg. "But I thought we were going to enter together – make it a team effort?"

"What does it say in the rules?" asked Charly.

"Yes," said Hannah, flicking her long red hair back behind her ears. "Is there anything to say that we can't enter together? That way we could design a complete wardrobe of clothes that all co-ordinate with each other."

"Cool!" said Flo, popping her thumb in her mouth as she started thinking some more about the outfit she wanted to design.

Meg flicked to the right page and started reading the rules of the competition.

". . .It doesn't say anything about a group entering," she said.

"What do you think we should do?" Zoe wondered, fiddling with her butterfly hairclip.

"Well," said Meg, smiling at her friend. "It doesn't say that we *can't*, does it? I think we should put in a group entry – a complete wardrobe of clothes designed with Glitter Girl style!"

"Brilliant!" Zoe grinned.

"Yes," agreed Charly. "That's a great idea!"

"Well," said Flo, "what are we waiting for? Let's get going!"

"What do we need to do?" asked Charly.

Meg read out the rules. "It says 'Entrants must design a complete outfit with accessories, including shoes'."

"Does that mean bags as well?" Zoe wondered.

"I think so," said Meg.

"Great!" said Flo. "So – how do we present our designs?"

Meg looked at the magazine again. "Umm – we need to draw our designs on a sheet of A4 paper, and put our names and addresses on the back. Oh – and we've got to send in a colour photograph of each of us as well!"

"What do they want those for?" Hannah wondered.

"To see if they think we'd make good models I suppose," said Charly.

"Well, we'd better get started then," said Meg.

"I've got lots of A4 sketch paper at home," said Flo. "I could go home and get it. And I can bring along some felt pens and pencils."

The girls agreed, and Flo dashed off home to pick up the materials they needed.

Ten minutes later there was a RAT-tat-tat! at the bedroom door.

"Who is it?" Hannah whispered from behind her bedroom door.

"GG!" came the reply. Hannah opened her bedroom door and Flo hurried in, carrying two huge carrier bags.

"I've brought a load of rough paper and my best block of paper," said Flo, pulling out a large pad of thick cartridge paper from one of the bags.

"Are you sure you don't mind us using it?" Charly asked.

"Course not – I mean you're only going to use one sheet each, aren't you?" said Flo. "We'll do our first sketches on the rough paper and then, when we're happy with everything, we can do our finished drawings."

"Right," said Meg, opening her notebook. "Who's going to design what?

"Bags I do the mini-skirt," said Hannah.

"Can I do dungarees?" asked Charly.

"Oh, I just can't decide. . ." said Flo, plaintively. ". . .OK, I think it's got to be the bootleg trousers and jacket."

Meg wrote it all down.

"And what will you do, Zoe?" she asked.

"I'm going to design a dress," Zoe said, already thinking of the great accessories that she could put with it.

"OK . . . I think I'd like to try a coat," said Meg.

"Sorted then!" said Flo. "Shall we get started?"

"Go Glitter!"

Chapter 2

Hannah's bedroom fell silent as the Glitter Girls began working hard on their designs. An hour or so later though, their creativity came to a temporary halt when Mrs Giles called them downstairs to the kitchen for tea.

Over slices of delicious pizza and glasses of fizzy apple juice, the Glitter Girls told Mrs Giles all about the competition.

"It sounds wonderful, girls," said Hannah's mum, as she sipped her mug of tea. "Have you all decided what you're going to design?"

"Yes," said Meg. "We're all working on our designs at the moment. And when we're happy with them, we're going to draw them all out properly on Flo's cartridge paper."

"And we've got to send off photographs of ourselves as well!" explained Charly.

"Are you going to send your school photographs?" asked Hannah's mum.

"No way!" said Zoe. "Mine's awful!"

"So's mine!" giggled Charly.

"I'm sure that's not true!" laughed Mrs Giles. "But I can see why you wouldn't want to send them in. So – what other photos have you got? How about using some from your holidays?"

"Well. . ." Flo murmured. "I don't really know. . ."

The Glitter Girls had been so busy discussing the designs for their outfits that they hadn't got as far as thinking about the photos.

"Well, I've got a camera," said Zoe. "We could take some photos ourselves."

"Yes, but . . . I don't want to be mean, Zoe. . ." Charly said, "but . . . well, it isn't exactly a professional camera, is it?"

Zoe laughed, not at all offended. "No, it isn't."

"I know!" said Meg, taking her notepad out of her pocket again. "We can get my dad to take them! He takes really good photos!"

"Great idea!" said Hannah.

"I'll ask him about it when he calls tomorrow night," Meg said, smiling.

"It all sounds very exciting," agreed Mrs Giles. "And – I was just wondering if you girls would like some help laying out your designs, I'd be very happy to lend a hand."

Hannah's mum made costumes for the local theatre, and her workroom was one of the Glitter Girls' favourite places.

"Thanks, Mrs Giles," said Charly. "That'd be great!"

"Yes," said Flo. "I remember when you did the designs for our ballet. You attached swatches of fabric to each design."

"That's right!" said Mrs Giles.

"Do you think that's how we should present our designs?" Hannah wondered.

"Oh yes!" said the other Glitter Girls, excitedly.

"It might make them stand out," said Mrs Giles.

"But how will we get hold of the type of fabric samples that Girl's Dream might want to use?" asked Flo.

"Well, you might not have exactly the same fabric – but you could give examples of the fabrics you'd like the garment made up in," suggested Mrs Giles.

"Cool!" said Zoe.

"But where would we get the fabric from?" Meg asked.

"Mum!" said Hannah, smiling, as she read her mother's thoughts.

Mrs Giles laughed. "I've got a huge basket filled with different fabric samples upstairs in my workroom," she explained. "I'm sure you'll find some good bits and pieces there."

"Brilliant!" said Flo, beaming at her friends.

"Do you think we could have a look now?"

Meg asked, anxious to get on with their project.

Mrs Giles laughed again. "Of course! If you've all had enough to eat?"

The Glitter Girls nodded. "Yes thanks, Mrs Giles, that was really nice!" said Zoe.

"OK," said Mrs Giles. "Why don't you go and get your sketch pads so that you can show me what kind of outfits you've got in mind? I'll meet you in my workroom."

"But we haven't finished drawing yet," explained Flo.

"That's OK," said Mrs Giles. "Perhaps the fabrics will inspire you to be even more creative!"

★ ♥ ★ ♥ ★ ♥ ★

Five minutes later, the Glitter Girls were seated at the huge table in the centre of Mrs Giles's workroom. On the walls were posters from the shows that she had worked on at the local theatre. There was also a large noticeboard that was covered in designs for the latest production.

"Here," said Mrs Giles, taking one of the illustrations off the board. "Look how this costume designer has presented her design. It's quite typical of the way it's done."

She put the design down on the table and sat down on one of the stools.

"She's put the name of the character at the top of the page," said Mrs Giles, "and then she's written captions explaining some of the detail that she wants me to reproduce on the costume itself."

The Glitter Girls could read things like "pencil pleats here" and "embroidery detail on yoke". The design had been coloured in with colouring pencils but even these were explained in writing by the designer who had emphasized that the green was to be "deep emerald" and that the headdress was to be "glittering, shimmering silver with jewelled detail".

"Wow!" said Flo, gently fingering the picture.

"Fantastic!" said Meg. "I want this costume!"

"Right," Mrs Giles laughed. "Shall we have a look through my basket and see if any of the fabric takes your fancy?"

"Go Glitter!" the girls replied.

Chapter 3

The Glitter Girls spent the rest of the afternoon looking through all kinds of wonderful fabrics in Mrs Giles's workroom.

"Look at this!" exclaimed Zoe, as she draped a piece of gossamer pink chiffon across her shoulder and admired her reflection in the mirror that hung behind the workroom door.

"It's lovely!" said Charly. "But how about this one?" She held up a swatch of purple and pink gingham. "It would be just right for a shirt, wouldn't it?"

"Yes, very cool!" agreed Zoe, who had chosen some purple fleece.

"Isn't this brilliant?" said Flo, clutching a piece of denim that was shot through with silver glitter. "It's almost the same as the fabric we saw in Girl's Dream!"

"Now," said Mrs Giles. "Why don't you work on your first sketches a little more, and add in some detail."

The Glitter Girls industriously got to work with their pencils.

"Wow!" said Mrs Giles, looking over Flo's shoulder. "I love the idea of that – it's like a kind of Glitter Girl cowboy outfit!"

With the glittery denim as her inspiration, Flo had designed a pair of jeans and a jacket, with a hat and handbag to match. The jacket had beads and jewels embroidered on the pockets.

"Hey, that's really cool!" said Charly, admiring her friend's work.

"I think I might have some beads and things that you could thread on to some cotton and attach to your designs to show what you mean," said Mrs Giles.

"Thanks!" said Flo, following Hannah's mum over to a little chest of drawers.

Between them, they found some purple and pink beads. As Flo threaded them on to a piece of cotton, Mrs Giles went over to see how the others were getting on. "That's great, Charly!" she said, leaning over Charly's shoulder to get a better look at her design.

"Thanks!" Charly beamed with pleasure.

"I really like the embroidery at the top of the dungarees. Why don't you create a smaller sketch in the corner of your finished design showing the pattern of your embroidered detail," suggested Mrs Giles.

"Good idea!" said Charly, immediately starting another sketch to do exactly that.

"And how are you getting on, Hannah?" Hannah's mum asked her daughter.

Hannah had designed a mini-skirt and jacket and had indicated that she wanted the jacket to be covered with badges.

"I like that touch," said Mrs Giles, pointing to the badges. "Are you going to attach your badges to the design?"

"Yes!" smiled Hannah, pleased.

Zoe's dress was totally cool too.

"I love the way you've designed it so that the skirt flares out on the bottom layer," said Mrs Giles. "And the way you've used contrasting fabrics on the different layers, too."

"Do you think I should show the pattern of the gingham on the design, in the finished drawing?" Zoe asked.

"Well," pondered Mrs Giles. "Perhaps you could use a soft colour to indicate it overall and then do one corner – say just here –" Mrs Giles pointed to one part of the design, "in more detail, to show the actual pattern. Then you can put a swatch of your fabric on the design and indicate what you mean."

"OK – cool," said Zoe, smiling with satisfaction.

Meg, inspired by the purple fleece fabric that

she had found, was busy designing a coat.

"That looks stylishly cosy!" said Mrs Giles. "I really like the way you've done the hood, Meg. The contrasting edge is really groovy."

"Thanks!" Meg grinned. "But what do you think I should do about the buttons, Mrs Giles?"

Hannah's mum smiled. "I think I've got just the thing!"

She hurried over to another one of her coloured workboxes and, after a few moments, fished out some fantastic purple transparent buttons. They had glitter suspended inside and they looked like jewelled sweets!

"Wow!" said Meg. "Should I attach one of these to my finished drawing?"

"Yes," said Mrs Giles. "Here's a little cellophane wallet to put it in. You can attach a corner of that to your design with a staple.

"Thanks!" Meg smiled, really pleased with how everything was going.

"Really, girls," said Mrs Giles. "I think your

designs are looking amazing. Once you've finished them all off, I'm sure you've got a great chance of winning the competition!"

"Go Glitter!" they all cried eagerly.

★ ♥ ★ ♥ ★ ♥ ★

By the end of the afternoon, the Glitter Girls had an impressive collection of designs to their credit.

"You've done brilliantly!" said Mrs Giles, genuinely impressed with the work they'd done that afternoon.

"It's been so much fun!" said Flo.

"And exhausting, too!" said Zoe.

"I know – but the hard work was worth it, wasn't it?" said Charly, as she looked over all of the designs that were spread out on the work table in front of them.

"I think you should present your work in a small portfolio," suggested Mrs Giles. "I'm sure I've got one at the theatre that we're not using at the moment."

"Thanks, Mum!" said Hannah, and the others nodded their heads in agreement.

"Now we've just got to persuade my dad to take our photographs," said Meg.

"Do you think he'll be OK about it?" Charly asked.

"Oh, I'm sure I can talk him round!" said Meg, with a twinkle in her eye.

Chapter 4

It was Monday morning and the Glitter Girls were in the playground at school.

"Did you get a chance to speak to your dad, Meg?" Zoe asked.

"I did," Meg replied, "and he reckoned that it should be OK. He's got a friend who owns a photographic studio in town – you know the place where you can go to have your passport photograph taken? Dad thinks he might be able to use the studio to take our photos."

"But won't that cost lots of money?" Charly wondered.

"No – Dad reckons that it'll be fine as long as we don't mind going at about six o'clock, after the studio's closed."

"Cool," said Flo. "So when will we know if it's happening?"

"Yes," said Hannah. "We've got to get our entries in quite soon now."

"Dad said he'd call me tonight. He's going to try and organize it for one night this week – maybe Wednesday," Meg replied.

"Great," said Zoe. "I can't wait!"

"Neither can I!" said Charly.

★ ♥ ★ ♥ ★ ♥ ★

On Tuesday morning, Meg arrived a bit late for school so the Glitter Girls weren't able to ask her if she'd heard from her dad until breaktime.

"So?" begged Zoe. "Any news?"

Meg smiled at her friends. "It's all arranged!" she said. "Tomorrow, as Dad said, at six o'clock."

"What should we wear?" Charly asked excitedly. "Not school clothes?"

"No way!" said Flo.

"I vote we wear our Glitter Girl T-shirts and jackets, don't you?" said Meg.

"Go Glitter!" the others agreed.

★ ♥ ★ ♥ ★ ♥ ★

By five-thirty on Wednesday afternoon, the Glitter Girls were totally organized for their photo shoot. They'd got together to change at Charly's house and had had a great time helping each other with their hair and nails.

"Time to get in the car, girls!" Mrs Fisher called up the stairs.

"Everyone got everything?" Meg asked.

"Go Glitter!" they all confirmed, and they ran downstairs to pile into Mrs Fisher's car.

It didn't take long to get to the studio and Meg's dad greeted them at the door.

"Hi Dad!" said Meg, giving him a hug.

"Hello, Mr Morgan!" chorused the other Glitter Girls.

"Well," said Mrs Fisher, smiling. "I think we'll

leave you girls to it and come back in about an hour when Lily and I have finished our shopping. OK?"

"Yes, thanks, Mrs Fisher," the girls said.

"See you later, then!" said Mr Morgan. Then he turned to the Glitter Girls. "Come on, let me introduce you to Steve." Steve was the owner of the studio.

"Great to have you here, girls," Steve smiled. "I'm going to help with the lighting and stuff while Meg's dad gets on with taking the shots."

"Shall we start, then?" Mr Morgan suggested. "I thought I'd take some individual shots and a group photo too. OK?"

"Go Glitter!" the girls replied, keen to get started.

The photo shoot had begun!

About an hour later, the shoot was over and the Glitter Girls were worn out! They'd smiled, laughed, jumped, sat, and stood, first on their own and then as a group.

"Did you enjoy that, girls?" asked Mr Morgan, as he tidied away the last of the equipment.

"It was great!" said Meg.

"Yes – thanks," said Hannah. "But modelling is hard work, isn't it?"

"When will we see the photos?" Zoe asked.

"I'll try to get them developed by tomorrow afternoon," said Mr Morgan. "I'll do contact sheets first. They're big sheets made up of all the individual photos. We'll use that to decide which are the best shots and then we'll only develop the good ones."

"Cool!" said Flo.

Just then, Mrs Fisher and Lily arrived.

"How did it go, girls?" Mrs Fisher asked. "Did you have a good time?" But she looked at the girls' smiling faces and quickly said, "I don't think I have to ask really, do I?"

The Glitter Girls laughed in response.

"It was fantastic!" said Charly, and the other girls nodded in agreement.

"I can't wait to see the pictures," said Hannah, grinning.

Mr Morgan smiled. "I'll pop round with the contact sheets after school tomorrow," he said. "See you then!"

"Thanks, Dad," said Meg. "We'll be at Hannah's tomorrow!"

"Yes – thanks!" added the others as they left to go home, tired but happy.

When Meg's dad arrived after school the next day, the Glitter Girls were still buzzing with excitement.

"What do they look like, Dad?" asked Meg, trying to grab the contact sheets out of her dad's hand.

Mr Morgan laughed. "Patience, Meg!" he said. "Now, where can we lay these out?"

"How about here on the kitchen table?" suggested Mrs Giles.

"Perfect!" said Mr Morgan, spreading out the sheets in front of the girls.

"Try not to get too many sticky finger marks on them, won't you!"

"Hey – these are really cool!" said Zoe when she saw the ones of the Glitter Girls all together.

"Should we use individual photos or a group one?" Flo asked.

"I think," said Meg, tucking her long curly blonde hair behind her ears, "that we should choose a single photo of each of us and then just one of us all together."

"Sounds good to me," agreed Zoe.

The others nodded.

"I like this one of me best," said Flo, pointing to a photo in which she was smiling.

Mr Morgan peered over her shoulder. "Yes – I think you're right, Flo. That's a great picture. Let me write down the number." Mr Morgan scribbled it down in his notebook and then turned to the others, "What about the rest of you?"

One by one, the remaining Glitter Girls each selected their favourite photo and then, together, they chose a photograph in which they were all punching the air in true "Go Glitter!" style.

"Right!" said Mr Morgan, gathering up the contact sheets. "I'll take these back to my darkroom and develop the shots you've chosen. I might develop a few more so that you've got extra copies to keep for yourselves too!"

"Thanks!" all the girls said at once.

"But will the pictures be ready by the end of the week, Dad?" Meg was worried that time was running out and they were getting close to the competition's closing date.

"Don't worry – I promise that I'll have them ready for the weekend!" said Mr Morgan, hugging his daughter affectionately.

"Go Glitter!" shouted the girls.

Chapter 5

RAT-tat-tat!

"Who is it?" whispered Flo.

"GG!"

It was Saturday, the day the Glitter Girls were going to send off their competition entry.

Flo opened her bedroom door and welcomed in Hannah, Zoe, Meg and Charly. They'd all come round to help get their entries together and ready to send off. And by late Saturday morning, the Glitter girls had done almost everything.

"So – photos?" asked Meg, checking everything off her list.

"Here!" said Hannah. "And I've put them in the portfolio Mum's given us."

"I've put the designs in," said Flo.

Meg ticked these off on her list. "And the entry form?"

"In the portfolio too," confirmed Zoe.

"Names and addresses on everything?"

"Yep!" Charly said.

"Then all we need is a signature from an adult and then we can post it!" Meg made a final tick in her notebook.

"Go Glitter!"

Every day for the next two weeks, the Glitter Girls rushed home from school, each hoping that they would find a letter about the Girl's Dream competition waiting for them. Every day they were disappointed.

But then something terrible happened which completely distracted the Glitter Girls from thinking about the competition.

One afternoon after school, Charly and Zoe

went off for their riding lesson as usual. But that night, Charly rang Flo, Hannah and Meg to tell them that the lesson hadn't gone exactly to plan.

"It's Zoe," Charly had explained to them. "She's had an accident . . . when we were riding. Zoe's pony bucked on her and she got thrown off. She got taken to hospital in an ambulance." She reassured each of the girls that her mum had rung Dr Baker, who'd said Zoe was fine, but that she had fractured her arm and would probably have to stay in hospital that night, but would be home tomorrow.

All the girls felt terrible for their friend and the next day at school they grilled Charly for more details.

"How did it happen?" Flo wanted to know.

"It was just an accident," Charly explained. "Her pony bucked while they were in the sand ring and Zoe lost her grip and came crashing down."

"Oh no . . . did the pony land on her?" asked Meg.

"I didn't see, but I don't think so," said Charly. "I expect she'd have been even more hurt if it had."

"I suppose she would," agreed Hannah. "Is she still in hospital now?"

"No, she's not," explained Charly. "Dr Baker spoke to Mum after I'd gone to bed and she said that Zoe did have to stay in overnight for observation. She was going home this morning though, and she's supposed to rest so she won't be at school, but Dr Baker wondered if we wanted to go and see her at her house after school today."

"Course we do!" the others said at once.

By breaktime, the whole school seemed to have heard about Zoe's accident.

"I think it would be a nice idea if everyone

made Zoe a 'Get Well' card, don't you?" suggested Miss Stanley when everyone was sitting quietly after silent reading.

The whole class agreed, and by the end of the afternoon, the Glitter Girls had quite a collection of messages and pictures to take to Zoe.

"Do you think Zoe's arm's in a sling?" Hannah wondered.

"I should think it's been bandaged or something," said Meg.

"When my sister broke her wrist, she had to have a plaster," Flo put in.

"Do you think that's what Zoe will have?" asked Charly.

"Probably," said Flo. "And we could sign it and draw pictures on it for her! That's what we did to Kim's."

The others laughed. There had to be something good to be found in their best friend's misfortune.

As soon as school was over, the girls rushed out, eager to get to Zoe's house. As usual, Charly's mum was waiting for them by the school gate.

"It's weird without Zoe, isn't it?" Mrs Fisher said when they were on their way. "It doesn't seem right without all five of you."

"I hope she's OK," Flo said with a concerned tone.

"She's probably a bit sore," Mrs Fisher said, "but I'm sure she's looking forward to seeing you."

"We've got lots of messages and cards for her," Meg said, and went on to explain about Miss Stanley's suggestion that everyone made cards.

"What a nice idea," said Mrs Fisher. "I'm sure they'll make Zoe feel lots better."

Pretty soon, the car was pulling up outside Zoe's house.

Dr Baker let them in, and the Glitter Girls

found Zoe sitting on the sofa in the living room, watching a video.

"Hi!" Zoe smiled, as she switched off the video with the remote. Fortunately her right hand was in full working order. But on her left arm, the Glitter Girls could see plaster running from just above her elbow down to her wrist. And the plaster was bright, dayglo pink!

"Hey! Groovy plaster, Zoe!" said Flo.

"Yeah, what a cool colour!" agreed Hannah.

"Isn't it good?" Zoe smiled.

"But doesn't it really hurt?" Meg asked.

"Not so much now that it's in plaster," said Zoe.

"So what happened?" asked Hannah. "I mean Charly told us that you got thrown off your pony, but how did it happen?"

"Well, we were going round the sand ring," Zoe explained, "and the pony in front of me suddenly stopped. I pulled my pony up but then there was this noise – I think someone dropped something in the yard, and it was really loud. Anyway, I think it must have scared my pony – I don't know . . . one minute I was sitting in the saddle asking her to stop and the next thing – SPLAM! I just went hurtling through the air and landed SMACK! on the sand." Zoe banged her right hand down on the sofa next to her to emphasize her fall.

"Did you get knocked out?" Flo asked.

"No," Zoe said. "But I did hit my head quite hard. That's why I had to stay in hospital last night – they thought I had concussion."

"Wow!" said Hannah. "Did you stay in the children's ward?"

"Eventually. I went to Accident and Emergency first and they did all these tests to check if I was OK. Then they X-rayed me and said it needed a plaster – I was really fed up. Until the doctor in the plaster room said that I could choose whatever colour plaster I liked! So, naturally, I chose pink!"

"Did you go up to the children's ward when the plaster was done?" asked Meg.

"Yes – but they let me come home after breakfast this morning," Zoe said, holding her plastered arm and admiring the colour again.

"I bet if Girl's Dream sold plaster casts they'd be that colour!" said Flo.

The others laughed.

"I wonder when we'll hear from Girl's Dream about the fashion show?" Hannah mused.

"I wonder *if* we will. . ." Meg sighed.

And so did all the others. . . But before they could get too depressed, Dr Baker came in.

"Who fancies something to eat?" she asked.

"Me!" the Glitter Girls all said at once.

Chapter 6

After another day at home, Zoe was well enough to go back to school. The Glitter Girls still hadn't heard anything from Girl's Dream. By the following week, the Glitter Girls had almost given up hope. But as they came out of school one afternoon, they saw Charly's mum standing by her car waving an envelope at them.

"I think this might be what you've been waiting for!" said Mrs Fisher excitedly, as the girls ran to meet her.

Charly grabbed the envelope from her mother and ripped it open.

"What does it say?" Flo asked, as Charly began reading the letter.

"Yes!" screamed Charly, jumping up and down. "Yes!"

"Yes what?" asked Meg impatiently.

Charly smiled. "It says that our entry has won us a place in the fashion show! We've got to go to London for the weekend to take part, and the show's at the Natural History Museum!"

"Go Glitter!" the girls all screamed, raising their arms above their heads. But Zoe, with her arm in plaster, could only raise one arm!

When the girls had calmed down a bit, Meg realized that Zoe wasn't looking her normal cheery self.

"What's wrong, Zoe?" she asked, concerned.

"It's this!" said Zoe, waving her plastered arm gently. "How can I take part in a fashion show with this?"

"Don't worry, there must be a way to sort it!" said Meg. "I'm sure!"

"Maybe you should have a word with your mum?" suggested Flo.

"Maybe. . ." said Zoe and she slumped into a seat in Mrs Fisher's car, not looking at all convinced.

★ ♥ ★ ♥ ★ ♥ ★

All of the Glitter Girls had letters similar to Charly's waiting for them when they got home that night. They screamed so loudly with excitement that the whole estate must have known the Glitter Girls had got some good news!

When Zoe got home though, her mum could see that something was wrong.

"What's up, love?" Dr Baker asked.

"It's the fashion show," Zoe explained, holding up her letter for her mum to see. "We've all been invited to go along to London."

"But that's great, isn't it?" Dr Baker was concerned.

"It would have been," sighed Zoe, "if I didn't have a fractured arm."

"Try not to worry about it too much, sweet-heart," Dr Baker tried to reassure her daughter.

"Well, whoever saw a fashion model with a broken arm?" Zoe despaired.

"Hmm. . ." Dr Baker said thoughtfully. "I see what you mean."

"It's just not fair!" said Zoe tearfully. "It would be just awful if the others got to go and I didn't!"

"It may not come to that, Zoe," Dr Baker said. "Perhaps you could go along and watch. . . That would still be good fun – wouldn't it?"

Dr Baker didn't sound that convinced herself. Zoe certainly wasn't.

"A bit, I suppose . . . but not much!"

Dr Baker put her arm around Zoe and carefully, so as not to hurt her arm, she gave her a hug.

"Tell you what, Zoe," she said. "Why don't I ring Girl's Dream and explain about your arm and see what they say?"

"Oh, yes Mum! Can you do it now?" Zoe begged.

Dr Baker laughed and looked at her watch. "OK – I suppose now is as good a time as any. Why don't you start your homework while I make the call. It will give you something to do."

Zoe tried to – but she just couldn't concentrate. She wanted to be in the fashion show with her friends so much! In fact, Dr Baker returned to the living room only a few minutes later.

"Did you get through?" Zoe implored. "What did they say?"

"I spoke to a really nice girl," Dr Baker explained. "She was really sorry to hear about your accident and hoped that you would feel better soon."

"But did she say that I could still go?" Zoe desperately wanted to know!

"She said she'd have to discuss it with her colleagues." Dr Baker put her arm round her daughter again.

Zoe sighed, she couldn't bear to wait much longer. . .

★ ♥ ★ ♥ ★ ♥ ★

On Friday afternoon, Dr Baker met the Glitter Girls from school as usual. She had a smile on her face, and Zoe knew immediately that it could only mean good news.

"Did the girl from Girl's Dream ring? What did she say, Mum? Can I still go? Can I be a model?" Zoe said anxiously.

"Well, they said they really want you to come along to the weekend," Dr Baker explained. "Only they may not be able to let you take part in the fashion show itself. They're worried about you doing more damage to your arm, especially with all the quick costume changes."

"Oh!" said Zoe, pleased that she was going with the others, but disappointed that she might not be able to have as much fun as them.

"But it'll still be the five of us!" said Hannah, putting her arm around her friend.

"Yes!" replied Zoe.

"Go Glitter!" her friends shouted.

There was another week to go before the fashion show weekend and the Glitter Girls spent every free evening trying on outfits and trying to decide what they should wear to London. In the end, they chose their jeans and their special Glitter Girl T-shirts and jackets!

At last, it was Friday afternoon, and the Glitter Girls were on their way! They were catching the train to London accompanied by Flo's and Meg's dads as well as Mrs Giles, Mrs Fisher and Dr Baker.

After rushing home from school to get changed, the girls whizzed off to the station, where they waited impatiently for their train.

"Here it is!" shouted Flo as she watched

the train pulling in at the other end of the platform.

The girls hugged each other excitedly. Their London adventure was about to begin!

Chapter 7

As soon as the Glitter Girls and their parents arrived in London, they took a taxi to their hotel, as instructed in their letters from Girl's Dream. They were greeted at reception by a young woman called Rose. It turned out that it was Rose who Dr Baker had spoken to about Zoe's arm.

"Hello everybody!" Rose beamed at them. "Well, you don't need any introduction, do you?" she smiled, looking at the Glitter Girls' outfits. "Now, which of you is which?"

Rose looked down at her clipboard. "I can see you must be Zoe!" she said, pointing to the plaster on Zoe's arm. "That's an amazing plaster you've got there!"

Zoe smiled and then Rose ticked her name off the list. The others called out their names and Rose ticked them off too.

"We've organized a party for all of the winners at seven o'clock," Rose went on. "So you've just got time to settle into your rooms."

"OK!" they all smiled.

★ ♥ ★ ♥ ★ ♥ ★

After being shown to their rooms, Hannah, Zoe, Meg, Flo and Charly met up with Dr Baker by the lift. The girls were sharing two rooms between them and their various parents had adjoining rooms that all linked up.

"Isn't everything here fantastic?" Flo gasped.

"It's brilliant!" agreed Hannah.

"So cool!" added Meg.

"So are you enjoying it here so far, girls?" Dr Baker asked the five best friends.

"Yes!" they all replied.

Charly looked down at her watch.

"Come on!" she said, beginning to panic. "Let's get going! I don't want to miss a thing!"

The party was in a big room in the hotel. Inside, it was decorated with balloons and streamers – everything was pink and purple, just like the inside of a Girl's Dream shop. Some of the other prize winners had already arrived and when Rose greeted everyone at the door as they came in, she gave them a big badge shaped like a heart which had each girl's name on.

The latest Robbie Williams track was playing and it was impossible for them not to start tapping their feet to the beat.

"Isn't this place great?" Hannah said.

"Yeah! I love the way they've decorated it," Zoe sighed.

"There are lots of other girls here," Meg commented.

"I wonder what kind of outfits they designed?" Flo said.

"Let's get chatting and find out!" said Charly, marching over to a group of girls who were standing by the food.

The Glitter Girls loved being at the party. Once they got chatting, they found out that the other girls had come from all over the country and the Glitter Girls soon realized how lucky they were because, unlike everyone else, they had come together and were with their best friends. All the other girls had just come with one of their parents.

As the party got going, everyone relaxed and the Glitter Girls found out that some of the girls had done some modelling before; they were keen to hear all about it. Everyone in the room was wearing something really cool. Obviously all the girls at the fashion show loved clothes just as much as the Glitter Girls because they'd all dressed up for the occasion, just like them.

After they munched their way through some delicious goodies and had a bit of a dance,

Rose clapped her hands and the room fell silent. Another girl handed each model-to-be a sheet of paper.

"Sorry to stop you all while you're having such fun," Rose apologized, and she smiled at all the girls in the room. "This is your timetable for tomorrow, ladies. It's going to be a busy day, so make sure you get your beauty sleep tonight!"

Everyone laughed, and Rose continued. "Now, I've got something special for all of you." Rose bent down and pulled something out of a huge cardboard box that was at her feet. She held up a big, bright pink folder that had Girl's Dream written on it. "There's one of these for each of you to take home – a souvenir of your time here this weekend, from all of us at Girl's Dream."

Everyone clapped as the folders were handed out to all the girls.

Like the others, the Glitter Girls eagerly

opened the folder to discover what was inside. There was Girl's Dream notepaper, pens and pencils; a badge which read *Girl's Dream Fashion Show*; a catalogue of the clothes that the girls were going to be modelling, and a special photo frame as well.

"There are going to be lots of photos taken on Sunday, girls," Rose explained. "So we thought that you would like the frame for your special souvenir photo! Now, I think you should all be going back to your rooms soon and getting that beauty sleep!"

"Go Glitter!" the five friends said to themselves. And straight away they started to look at the gorgeous clothes in the catalogue.

Chapter 8

In fact it turned out to be really hard to get to sleep that night. It had been such a brilliant day that it was difficult to stop talking about everything that had happened and what was going to happen next! On top of that, because the Glitter Girls were in adjoining rooms they were in the middle of what was turning out to be a great sleepover!

In the end, Mr Eng and Mr Morgan came into one of the girls' bedrooms at the same time as Dr Baker and Hannah's and Charly's mums came into the other.

"For goodness' sake, you lot! When are you going to be quiet?" Mr Eng asked.

"I really do think that you need to get some sleep, girls," said Mrs Giles.

At first, the Glitter Girls had been talking so much that they didn't even hear anyone come in. Charly and Flo were in the middle of a bed-bouncing competition!

"Get down from there immediately, you two!" Mrs Fisher said in a loud voice.

The two of them were so taken by surprise that they nearly fell off the beds! Shame-faced with embarrassment, Flo and Charly stumbled off the beds and stood staring at their parents.

"Sorry," said Flo, popping her thumb into her mouth.

"Oops!" exclaimed Charly, eventually getting her balance back and sitting down on the bed.

"We're really sorry. . ." said Meg, already starting to clear up the messy beds that surrounded them.

"Right, time to go to sleep, girls. I mean it," said Charly's mum.

"Yes," agreed Mr Morgan. "Rose told us how

much you've got to do tomorrow. I think it's definitely time to turn the lights out."

"It's OK," said Hannah, feeling embarrassed to have been caught making such a noise. "We'll tidy up."

"Don't worry," said Dr Baker, "we'll help you get this lot straight. And I think we ought to take away some of these plates of food."

"Or what's left of it!" laughed Mrs Fisher.

A few minutes later, the room was looking more respectable.

"Right – in bed, you lot!" said Mr Eng.

The Glitter Girls did exactly what they were told, and slipped under their duvets.

"See you in the morning!" said their parents.

"Night," the Glitter Girls replied, as their lights were switched off.

In fact, they were so tired they couldn't remember going to sleep. It just happened – and the next thing they knew it was morning!

★ ♥ ★ ♥ ★ ♥ ★

Despite eating so much the night before, the Glitter Girls were ravenously hungry, and tucked in to a huge breakfast before joining everyone else back down at the room where the party had been.

Rose met everyone at the door and smiled at them.

"Morning! Right, we'd like the five of you to join in with a class."

"A class?" Meg asked, puzzled.

"Yes – you're going to be coached on walking down the catwalk," Rose explained.

"Go Glitter!" the five girls cheered happily, and went over to the other side of the room, where a number of the other girls were already waiting.

Soon after, Rose came over to them.

"OK, I think everyone's here now. The first thing we want you all to have a go at is walking down the catwalk. Terri Stafford, from Stafford's modelling school is here to give you all some help."

"It looks a bit tatty, doesn't it?" Meg whispered,

as she looked at the wooden staging, laid out in a kind of T shape. The room certainly didn't bear any resemblance to the decorated room where they'd had the party the night before.

"Yes," agreed Hannah. "But I'm sure everything will look better at the museum."

"Oh yes," said Flo.

Rose introduced all the girls to Terri, who was wired up to a microphone system and had a thin headset with a tiny mouthpiece.

"Hello, girls!" Terri smiled at them all. "Now let's see what you all look like – spread out a bit!"

Terri walked up and down the group of girls until she got to Zoe.

"Ah, yes!" Terri said. "You're the girl who's broken her arm! Zoe, isn't it?"

Zoe blushed – she hadn't wanted to stand out from everyone else but now her plaster was making sure that she did!

"Never mind, Zoe," Terri smiled. "Perhaps you'd like to be first down the catwalk? I want to see how well you can cope with that plaster of yours. By the way, I love the colour!"

Go first? Zoe was terrified. But it seemed that Terri could read her mind.

"Don't worry – it's not so bad!" said Terri. "Why don't I go down once and show you what I want you to do? Cue music, please!" Terri called into the mouthpiece.

Straight away, Atomic Kitten's latest single blared out around the room. Terri bounced up the stairs and on to the catwalk. Then she strolled down the T shape with one hand on her hip until she got to the bottom, stopped, waved and turned to come back.

"OK, girls?" Terri said to all of them. "You can do that, can't you?"

"Yes!" they all replied, already moving to the music.

"Come on then, Zoe!" Terri beckoned her on to the catwalk. "Show me how well you can do with that plaster!"

Fortunately, Zoe had got used to her plaster by now and could do most things (except riding) pretty much as normal, so she didn't really notice the plaster as she bopped her way down the catwalk.

"You're a natural, Zoe!" Terri smiled. "Well everyone – see if you can do it like Zoe! Keep your heads up!" Terri called to them all. "Smile! Go on, girls, enjoy yourselves! If you look like you're having fun then so will everyone in the audience!"

Zoe had no trouble at all in smiling! To be told that she was a natural at modelling by someone like Terri almost made her forget that she had her plaster at all!

Terri had three other girls helping her and all four of them spent the morning helping every-one to perfect their walk down the catwalk. Terri explained that there should only ever be two girls on the catwalk at the same time. But they also had to make sure that there was never a time when no one was on the stage. They also had to follow a one-way system so that no one bumped into anyone!

It was hard work and the Glitter Girls didn't get a chance to chat with each other during the whole rehearsal. By lunchtime, the girls were happy but exhausted! They were quite relieved to sit down to a picnic on the floor of the big room and eat and chat with the others.

"How's it going, girls?" Rose asked the entire group.

"Great!" was the general response.

"Good!" Rose checked her clipboard. "Now, this afternoon we'd like you to try on the clothes, so enjoy your break, and we need you to be ready for two o'clock."

The Glitter Girls, who were sitting together, hugged each other.

"Isn't this fantastic?" Meg asked.

"Go Glitter!" the others whispered in response.

Chapter 9

After their lunch and a brief chat with their parents, the Glitter Girls congregated with the others in the room, as instructed.

"OK, girls." Rose consulted her clipboard. "When I call out your name, can you please go over to the other girls –" she pointed to Terri's helpers from earlier, who were standing next to two long rails laden with gorgeous clothes – "who will help you to find the outfits we've chosen for you. We need to check that everything fits!"

Trying on the outfits was the bit that Zoe had been dreading. After all – how could she climb into some of the things if they didn't have buttons or a wide enough neck for her to get her plaster cast through?

Fortunately, Terri and Rose seemed to have anticipated these problems.

"We thought you ought to wear the same T-shirt throughout, Zoe – because of the quick changes. Then all you need to do is swap jackets and trousers or skirts."

"Thanks!" said Zoe. "Great idea!"

Rose smiled. "And I will ask one of Terri's assistants to be around to help you with zips and stuff!"

Meg smiled at Zoe. Like the other Glitter Girls, she was so relieved that Zoe hadn't had to miss out on an adventure as exciting as this fashion show was turning out to be!

Rose explained to everyone that they were the outfits that would be on sale in Girl's Dream next season. The fashion show was going to be a preview for the newspapers and magazines so that they could write about them in their next issues!

"Isn't this just great?" Flo exclaimed.

"It's brilliant," agreed Hannah.

"I never thought I'd be able to do this!" said Zoe.

"I'm so pleased you could come!" said Meg, as she slipped on a pair of trousers.

"We all are!" smiled Hannah, and the other Glitter Girls all voiced their agreement.

The clothes were amazing! There were skirts – long and short, all different colours and fabrics – fabulous jeans with neon patterns on them. There were party dresses, coats and lots of different types of jackets – and each of the Glitter Girls wanted to take all of the clothes home with them. Just like every other girl there!

An hour or so later, everyone had tried on the various items of clothing that had been selected and once everything was labelled and back on its hanger, Terri called the rehearsal to a close.

"Time for tea break, girls!" Rose explained. "But we need you back here at five for another run through so that we can work out in which order each of you will be on!"

"Go Glitter!" the Glitter Girls called. And everyone around them wanted to join in, too.

★ ♥ ★ ♥ ★ ♥ ★

The final rehearsal of the day was exhausting. Rose and Terri's helpers showed all of them how to locate their outfits quickly and explained that if they had all the zippers and buttons undone, then they could slip into the clothes really quickly.

"We will help with the zipping up and stuff," offered Rose, sensing that Zoe was still nervous about that bit.

It was hard work, but great fun, and by the end of it, each of the girls was fairly certain that she knew who she followed and what she should be wearing.

"Now, tomorrow morning, I want you all down here at nine o'clock sharp," explained

Rose. "You'll have another catwalk session to check that you know your order. Then you'll have your hair done before you are bussed over to the Natural History Museum. Once we're there, there will be just enough time for a quick lunch and then another rehearsal before you have your make-up done and the fashion show starts."

"OK, girls?" Terri asked.

OK? It sounded fantastic! And Terri could tell that just by looking at the faces of the girls in front of her.

Dr Baker was there to meet the Glitter Girls at the door.

"Did you have a great time, girls?" she asked.

"Brilliant!" they all replied.

"Well – how about we go out for a pizza this evening?" Dr Baker asked.

"Go Glitter!" came the universal reply!

Chapter 10

The girls reported at nine o'clock the next morning for the run through.

"Don't worry too much about getting confused," Terri and Rose reassured everyone. "After all, there'll be people to help you!"

The Glitter Girls loved all the music that had been chosen as the soundtrack to the fashion show. They recognized all the latest chart hits – Westlife, Robbie, Kylie, Blue, Britney Spears – and it made them feel great to walk down the catwalk to them all.

They remembered all Terri's advice about how to walk confidently and make the clothes look great that she'd taught them the day before.

"Keep smiling, girls!" Terri encouraged them. "And move to the music."

One by one they bounced down the catwalk, enjoying the music and counting out their steps.

"I love this," said Charly, as she finished her turn.

"It's so much fun, isn't it?" Flo whispered back.

And as each of the Glitter Girls had a chance to go through their swirl along the catwalk, they agreed too.

As soon as the rehearsal was over, Rose whisked everyone over to a team of hairdressers in the next room. Each of them got the chance to sit down in front of a huge mirror surrounded by lights. Then they had their hair curled, braided and brushed into fantastic styles. The Glitter Girls just loved having so much attention – it reminded them of their own Magical Makeover at the school fête!

"Hey, you look great!" said Hannah, when she saw the way Meg's hair had been sprayed with a glittery hairspray.

"Thanks," smiled Meg. "I love it!"

"Wow! You all look fantastic!" said Terri, walking over to them. "Your mums and dads are going to be so proud of you, aren't they?"

Everyone grinned. The Glitter Girls were really pleased that some of their parents had come with them, but they wished that all of their mums and dads, and their brothers and sisters, could have come too.

"Right," said Rose looking at her watch. "There's just time for everyone to have a drink before we head off to the museum!"

★ ♥ ★ ♥ ★ ♥ ★

None of the Glitter Girls had been to the Natural History Museum before, and Zoe, especially, had always wanted to visit. She was mad about animals! And when they arrived at the museum, she wasn't disappointed.

There were models and skeletons of animals everywhere, and a huge moving dinosaur in the main hall! The Glitter Girls loved it all. After they'd finished their picnic lunch they had a short while to look round before they made their way to a room off one of the galleries that had been closed especially for the Girl's Dream fashion show.

The girls couldn't believe their eyes when they arrived! There was the catwalk that they had been rehearsing on at the hotel, only now it was draped with silver material that had GIRL'S DREAM written all over it in bold pink lettering. There were lights positioned all around the stage and shining down on the catwalk. And Meg noticed that there was a spotlight positioned up in the balcony that surrounded the impressive room.

"Wow!" said Flo, mightily impressed with what she saw.

"Isn't this great?" agreed Charly.

"It's fab!" said Hannah.

"Cool!" exclaimed Meg and Zoe together.

"Hello, girls," said Rose, greeting them at the door of the gallery. "Can you pop over there and put on your first outfit? We start the dress rehearsal in ten minutes!"

The Glitter Girls made their way to the chaotic backstage area behind the catwalk, where they changed into their outfits and joined the other girls in the queue by the catwalk steps as the music started up. It had been decided that the youngest girl, who was only six, should start the show, and she strode down the catwalk with a beaming smile!

"Come on, girls!" encouraged Terri. "Keep your heads up!"

The final rehearsal had begun.

When it was over, Terri came up on the

catwalk and congratulated all of the girls.

"You did fantastically well, girls!" she said. "And as for you, Zoe – brilliant! I think a pink plaster is going to become an essential on the catwalk next season – all the models are going to want one."

Everyone laughed, especially Zoe, who was relieved to get Terri's approval.

"Now, there's someone here who wants to talk to you too!"

A very tall, elegant-looking girl with long dark hair stood up from one of the chairs that had been laid out around the catwalk, and walked over towards the girls.

"That's Katya!" exclaimed Hannah.

"Who?" asked Flo.

"You know!" said Meg. "She's a supermodel!"

"Oh yes!" said Charly.

"Hello, young ladies!" Katya said. "I'm so impressed with your modelling – you all look amazing up there."

Everyone grinned back enthusiastically.

"I'm so looking forward to seeing you in the final show," Katya went on. "You all did so well just now. I really enjoyed it!"

"Now, before you all go to have your final make-up done," said Terri, looking at her watch and conscious that time was flying by, "I want you all to see Katya come down the catwalk!"

Everyone burst into applause as Katya climbed the steps and sauntered along the catwalk, just like they had done. Only Katya never once looked like she was having to think about what she was doing. And she even winked at them when she got to the end!

The Glitter Girls were determined to try to be like Katya – but would they manage it?

"Now," said Rose. "Has anyone got any questions for Katya before you all to zoom off to have your make-up done?"

A sea of hands shot up.

"Let's start with you," said Rose, pointing to one of the youngest girls.

"Did you always want to be a model?" she asked.

"Yes!" said Katya. "And I had my first chance when I was about your age too – in a competition, a bit like this!"

After that, questions were fired at Katya by all the girls. Then the Glitter Girls got their chance. How long had she been modelling? Did she travel all over the world? Did she have a whole wardrobe of fantastic outfits?

"Are you always going to be a model?" Meg wanted to know.

"For a little while yet," Katya confirmed. "But I've been thinking about going back to school – you know, college. I'd like to be a teacher."

"A teacher?" Meg beamed. "That's what I want to be!"

"Well – perhaps we'll end up in the same school!" smiled Katya.

"I'm afraid we're going to have to stop there," said Rose. "Come on, girls – time for make-up!"

★ ♥ ★ ♥ ★ ♥ ★

Once more the girls made their way backstage where they approached the rails of clothes, already waiting for them.

"Put your first outfit on now, girls," Rose instructed. "If you're thirsty, have one last sip of water before you put on a make-up cloak. You can't drink after you've had your lips glossed!"

It was great being made-up. There was a large team of make-up artists and they all had huge boxes filled with every colour of lip gloss, nail polish and eyeshadow you could imagine. And, of course, all of it came from Girl's Dream.

In fact, they didn't end up with huge amounts of make-up each. But they did have a very pretty touch of glittery eyeshadow, a sweep of glitter on their cheeks and a dab of lip gloss.

"You look great!" said Meg to the others.

"So do you!" they all replied at once.

"You certainly do," said Rose, as she came over to them. "But come on! No time to chat! The show starts in fifteen minutes, so can everyone take their positions behind the curtains, please!"

The Glitter Girls did as they were told and excitedly took their places behind the curtains. How they wished all of their families could be there to see them!

As they nervously chatted with the other girls, the Glitter Girls became aware that the room outside was filling with people.

"Hey – there's a tiny gap in the curtain!" said Zoe, pointing it out to her friends.

"Can you see through it?" Hannah asked. "Is it packed out there?"

Zoe peeked through. "Hey, I can! Wow – there's my mum! And your dad, Flo!"

"Let me see!" said Flo. "Hey – there's my sister too! And Meg's brother! Everyone *is* here!"

The Glitter Girls all looked through the tiny slit in the curtain.

"Go Glitter!" they all cheered as loudly as they dared.

★ ♥ ★ ♥ ★ ♥ ★

"Everyone ready? Cue music! Go!"

Terri started the music and the fashion show had begun!

"Go Glitter!" the girls grinned at each other. This was going to be such fun!

Chapter 11

It seemed like no time at all before the show was over. Their time on the catwalk had disappeared in a flash of cameras and applause! At the end, all of the girls stood behind the curtains hugging each other in excitement.

"Shussh! Girls!" Rose whispered. "There's some announcements to be made!"

A man stepped on to the catwalk and introduced himself. His name was Mr Alexander and he was the managing director of Girl's Dream.

"First of all, I'd like to welcome on to the stage all the wonderful young ladies who have modelled for us today!"

Rose ushered all of them out from behind the curtains. Standing on the stage, the Glitter Girls were dazzled by the flashes coming from the cameras of the row of photographers sitting near the front of the stage.

The man from Girl's Dream carried on talking. "I think you will all agree that we have seen some great talent and some wonderful clothes here today."

There was lots of applause from the audience, who all seemed to agree with him. On the stage, all of the girls were beaming with happiness.

"Now, there is one more thing to tell you all," Mr Alexander went on. "As you know, all the clothes you've seen here this afternoon are from our next collection. But there is one outfit that we haven't yet shown you, and that's the winning outfit from our design competition!"

All of the girls gasped. In the excitement of the fashion show, they'd forgotten that one of the outfits was going to be chosen as the overall winner and made up to be sold in Girl's Dream!

Mr Alexander continued. "So, it gives me great pleasure to ask Katya to come on the catwalk and unveil the winning design, which I am sure you will agree is fantastic!"

There was thunderous applause as Katya stepped up on to the catwalk. She said a few words to the audience and then walked over to a mannequin which had been covered in the same silvery material that adorned the catwalk. With a flourish, Katya pulled off the fabric, to reveal a girl-sized mannequin, wearing an amazing jean and jacket set.

"Flo – that's your outfit!" exclaimed Meg.

"It is!" screamed Hannah.

"Wow!" yelled Charly.

"Well done!" squealed Zoe, hugging Flo with her one free arm.

"Now," said Mr Alexander, as the applause died down. "I'd like to ask our other winning model – the one who designed this outfit – to come forward, please. Flo Eng!"

Flo stood stock still, totally speechless. Had he really said her name? Was that really her outfit? There must be some mistake!

"Go Glitter!" the Glitter Girls screamed.

But still Flo stood there, not moving.

"Go on, Flo!" Meg pushed Flo forwards towards Katya and Mr Alexander. "You've won!"

★ ♥ ★ ♥ ★ ♥ ★

The applause seemed to go on for ever once Flo had stepped forward. And no one could have been more proud of Flo than her fellow Glitter Girls.

"Isn't it brilliant?" Meg said, when they were back behind the stage again.

"I can't believe it!" said Flo, clutching the special gift that she had been given as her prize. Her own outfit made up in her own size, especially for her!

"This has been some adventure!" sighed Charly.

"Go Glitter!" her friends agreed.

But after they had changed back into their own clothes it was time to go home, and the Glitter Girls said goodbye to all their new friends as well as Rose and Terri.

"We'll look forward to seeing you on the catwalk again some time!" called Rose, as they piled into their taxis and she waved them off.

"Well, did you have loads of fun?" asked Mrs Giles.

"It was the best," said Hannah.

And her friends agreed.

There were so many people accompanying the Glitter Girls on the train home that they almost took up a whole carriage!

"I wish I'd got to talk to Katya – she's gorgeous," said Meg's brother, Jack.

"Hey," said Meg. "Have you got a crush on her?"

"Jack! You've gone all red!" Flo said loudly – so loudly that everyone else who was with them stopped talking and looked at Jack.

"Stop it!" Jack yelled and covered his face – which was so red it looked like it was on fire – with his arm.

Everyone laughed.

"She is gorgeous," said Beth, who was one of Zoe's sisters. She felt sorry for Jack because he was so embarrassed. "Everyone thinks so."

"But how come you all got to be here, anyway?" Zoe asked, wanting the mystery solved finally.

"We couldn't miss out on seeing you lot on the catwalk, could we?" explained her other sister, Jemma.

"So we got an early train this morning and came down to London," said Beth.

"Yes, and you were all great," said Flo's sister, Kim. "I was dead proud of you."

"Thanks, Kim," Flo smiled, pleased that her sister really thought that.

"We're all proud of you!" said Mrs Fisher, and all the other mums and dads agreed with her.

The Glitter Girls were so happy that they sat on the train in a kind of glittery glow, unable to stop smiling.

"So what's it like being a model then?" Dr Baker wanted to know. "Do any of you want to do that when you leave school?"

"It was really good fun," Charly confirmed.

"It was excellent!" agreed Hannah. "But I don't think I want to be a model when I leave school. I still want to be a ballerina."

"And I still want to drive fast cars!" said Flo.

"Go Glitter!" said Lily, Charly's baby sister, raising her arms in the air, just like she'd seen the Glitter Girls do so many times.

"Go Glitter!" the whole carriage replied, and everyone laughed.

Tired but still excited about their brilliant time, the Glitter Girls spent the rest of their journey home telling all their families everything about their fantastic fashion show weekend.

It had been a great Glitter Girl adventure, but the Glitter Girls soon settled back into their routine.

A couple of weeks after the fashion show, Mrs Fisher met them after school with a final surprise. She was waving something at them, just like she had when Charly's letter had arrived telling them that they were in the fashion show.

"What is it, Mum?" Charly asked, hurrying over.

"Look at this!" Mrs Fisher smiled, handing them a copy of a magazine.

It was the latest issue of *Girl's Dream*. And it had a picture of the Glitter Girls on the front – at the fashion show!

"Go Glitter!" they all screamed at once!

Don't miss:

Spooky Sleepover

The Glitter Girls were sitting in Meg's kitchen when the back door was flung open and Meg's brother Jack tumbled in, followed by his friend Nick.

"Hi, you lot." Jack dumped his PE kit down by the door and grabbed two glasses from the cupboard. "Got any food?" he asked as he poured some milk into the glasses and handed one of them to Nick.

"Help yourself to some pizza," said Meg, pushing the plate in the boys' direction.

"So, what are you girls up to?" Nick asked the Glitter Girls. Like Jack, he used to go to the same school as the Glitter Girls, so he knew them quite well.

"Just talking and hanging out," said Charly, twiddling with her hair.

"Yes," added Hannah. "We were just wondering what we might get up to this weekend, but we haven't decided yet."

"What are you two doing?" Zoe asked.

"Oh, we're off to the Energy Zone tonight – down at the community centre," Jack explained.

"What's that?" Flo asked.

"It's a youth club," explained Meg. "They go every Monday and Friday night."

"Cool!" said Hannah. "Can we come?"

"No way!" said Nick.

"Why not?" Charly asked. "Can't girls come?"

"No!" said Jack.

"That's not true!" exclaimed Meg. "Sue used to go!"

"So did Jemma and Beth!" added Zoe. "They always had a brilliant time there."

"So why can't we go then?" Flo wanted to know.

Jack and Nick stuffed more pieces of pizza in their mouths and stood leaning against the kitchen worktops, laughing with each other like they were sharing some kind of private joke.

Eventually, Nick said, "Well we just don't want you there tonight."

"Yes – we've got stuff to talk about with Danny," said Jack.

"What stuff?" asked Meg, irritated by her brother.

"And who's Danny?" demanded Charly, pushing her pink glasses back up her nose.

"Keep your hair on!" said Jack. "Danny's the bloke that runs Energy Zone."

"What are you going to be talking about?" Meg wasn't going to let her brother get away without explaining why the Glitter Girls couldn't go to the Energy Zone too!

"It's this sleepover," Nick said.

"Sleepover?" the girls exclaimed. They exchanged smiles – a sleepover was definitely something that they wanted to hear about!

"Where are you sleeping over?" Flo wanted to know.

"It's not tonight!" Jack said defensively. "We're just talking about it tonight."

"Well, when is it?" asked Meg.

"And where is it?" Hannah quizzed them.

"It's in a couple of weeks' time," Nick explained. "In the church tower at St Mildred's."

"Brilliant!" said Zoe.

"Yes," said Jack. "It's going to be cool. We're doing it to raise money for the mayoress's charity."

"For the African children's hospital!" said Charly.

"How did you know?" Nick exclaimed.

"We read about it in the paper," Hannah said smugly.

"It's a great idea," Meg said, sitting back in her chair with a thoughtful look on her face. "And I don't see why we shouldn't get to do it too!"

"No way!" said Jack quickly, looking to Nick for support.

"Not possible, girls!" added Nick. "You're just too titchy to come."

"How do you know?" said Meg.

Jack and Nick exchanged glances, desperately searching for a reason.

"See!" said Zoe.

"The sleepover's only for members of the Energy Zone," said Jack. "And anyway, it's probably full up by now. I'm sure there won't be any space for you lot."

"No," said Nick. "And you'd be too scared!"

"Scared?" Flo exclaimed. "Why? We've done loads of sleepovers!"

"Yes, but not in a church tower!" said Nick.

"A *haunted* church tower," added Jack. "Everyone knows the church has a ghost."

"I've never heard that before," said Flo, secretly wondering if what Jack had just said was true.

"Huh!" said Meg, determined not to be defeated by her brother when a great idea for a Glitter Girl adventure seemed to be within their grasp. "I think that we should go to the Energy Zone ourselves this evening to find out!"

"Go Glitter!" her four friends agreed enthusiastically, only a little bit worried about the thought of the church being haunted.

Jack and Nick looked at each other.

"Oh, *great*. . ." they both sighed.